LITTLE MISS SUNSHINE
and the **Three Bears**

Roger Hargreaves

Original concept by
Roger Hargreaves

Written and illustrated by
Adam Hargreaves

EGMONT

Little Miss Sunshine went for a walk in the woods.

And because it was a lovely hot day she decided to go for a long walk.

She walked.

And she walked …

Little Miss Sunshine settled down to wait, glad to be out of the storm.

Suddenly the door burst open and Mr Greedy barged his way in.

"Mr Greedy, what are you..." began Little Miss Sunshine, but before she could finish Mr Greedy spied the three bowls on the table.

"Ooh, Porridge!" he cried. "I'm starving!"

"You can't eat that porridge!" cried Little Miss Sunshine.

But Mr Greedy was hungry and he didn't listen.

The first big bowl he tried was too hot.

The next medium bowl was too cold.

But the last small bowl was just right.

So right that before Little Miss Sunshine knew it,
Mr Greedy had finished it all.

Mr Greedy looked at the small empty bowl.

"Well, that wasn't nearly enough for me," he said.
"I'm off to find a bigger meal," and he left as suddenly
as he had arrived.

Mr Greedy had hardly been gone a minute when the door was flung open for a second time and in stumbled Mr Clumsy.

"Hello, Mr Clumsy," said Little Miss Sunshine. "What brings you here?"

"Oooh, my poor feet!" he moaned. "I've been walking for miles. I need a rest."

And he went into the living room where there were three chairs.

"You can't come in here!" cried Little Miss Sunshine.

But Mr Clumsy didn't listen and he sat in the big chair.

It was too lumpy.

The medium chair was too soft.

But the small chair… well, the small chair was just right.

So right that Mr Clumsy leaned back, but being his usual clumsy self, he leaned back too far and with a loud **CRACK!** the chair broke.

Mr Clumsy jumped up and said that he had just remembered something he had to do very urgently.

And he left.

Poor Little Miss Sunshine.

She looked miserably at the broken chair.

What was she going to say to the three bears?

It was then that Little Miss Sunshine heard a loud, gruff voice coming from the kitchen.

"Who's been eating **my** porridge?" demanded the voice.

"Who's been eating **my** porridge?" asked the medium voice.

And then a tiny, squeaky voice said, "Who's been eating **my** porridge and eaten it all up?"

Then the three bears came into the living room.

"Who's been sitting in **my** chair?" said the big bear.

"Who's been sitting in **my** chair?" said the medium bear.

"And who's been sitting in **my** chair and broken it?" cried the little bear.

The three bears glared angrily at Little Miss Sunshine.

"Not me!" she cried.

Just then the door flew open for a third time. It was Mr Lazy.

"Aaargh," he yawned. "It's time for my nap! I need a bed!"

"You're not sleeping in **my** bed!" boomed the big bear.

"You're not sleeping in **my** bed!" said the medium bear.

"And you're not sleeping in **my** bed!" squeaked the little bear.

Mr Lazy's face fell.

"You can come and sleep at my house," said Little Miss Sunshine.

The bears were very happy to hear this, so Mr Lazy and Little Miss Sunshine said goodbye and set off back to her house.

However, as you know, it was a very long walk and Mr Lazy kept having to stop for a quick forty winks so it was very late when they finally arrived.

Late enough for it to be Little Miss Sunshine's bedtime too.

In fact it was everyone's bedtime.

Big bear was in his big bed.

Medium bear was in his medium bed.

Little bear was in his little bed.

Mr Lazy was tucked up in Little Miss Sunshine's bed.

And Little Miss Sunshine was ...

… on the sofa!

Poor Little Miss Sunshine.